P9-DIE-137

Z
Z
Z

For Simon & Casper, my new friends

Thank you to Andrice, Beth, Craig, Gene, Jesse(E), Jesse(R),
Rina, Shiga, Veronica, Kat and Clo-Clo

Published in the United States 2015 by
Blue Apple Books
515 Valley Street, Maplewood, NJ 07040
www.blueapplebooks.com

02/15
Printed in Korea
ISBN: 978-1-60905-394-9

1 3 5 7 9 10 8 6 4 2

Long Tail Kitty

Come Out and Play

by Lark Pien

BLUE APPLE

Magical Night

Where IS he???
The moon is already so high in the sky!

I'm waaaiting!

LONG TAIL KITTY!

huff!
huff!
Hiya, LTK!
Tony! Finally!
Oho! Are we in a hurry?
We are!

C'mon, I know a shortcut!
Lead the way!

Um... are you sure this is right?
The river is on the other side of these woods.

Hmm... spooky.
Relax! I know my way around these parts.

SO DO I!
yeep!
wah!

Big E! You joker! How did you get behind us?
With MAGIC!
Ha! You always say that.

I LOVE magic!
There's going to be a magic show on the ROBOBOAT tonight!
Are YOU going to go?
We ARE!
Let's go together!

Hop on board the Pachyderm Express, kitties!
toot toot!

To the riverfront!
trot
trot
trot!

There it is!
THE ROBOBOAT!

So sparkly!
I see giant milkshakes!
Is that a trampoline?!

Welcome to the ROBOBOAT!
Step on board for a night of deee-light!

Whoa! One minute there, my good sir!
? ? ?

You exceed the size limit, my friend!

But...
Elephants are TOO BIG for the Roboboat.
Ha-Ha! Slowpokes!
Tony, wait!
ZING!
Games 'n' fun, here I come!

Please go back the way you came.
But Robobarker, SIR, there is a magic show that I cannot miss!

Wait here, Big E!
I'm gonna get Tony. I'll be right back!

That Tony! Where did he go?

How do I find him when everyone in town is on this boat? TONY!!
?
who's TONY?

Sorry, Big E. I couldn't find Tony!
Big E?
Where did Big E go???
NOBODY THERE!

Geez, now I've lost Big E, too!

Wherever they are...

... I hope they're having fun.
Step right up! Step right up, kitties!

Try your hand at the Fishy Wishy Ring Toss! Win yourself a fish!
Tony needs to see this!

I guess I'll give it a try.
Thank you!

toss!
clink!
Oho! We have a winner!

Thanks for playing!
Tony would definitely like this game!

Who will water these thirsty beasts?
Big E would give this a go!

Winner!

Tony's milkshakes!
The first critter to finish keeps his mug!
glub!
slllllp!
Urp!

And is THIS the trampoline Big E saw? It's tiny!!

MY PALS SING MUCH BETTER THAN ME! OH! WHERE CAN THEY BE!?
Step down, please! I'll give you this sliding whistle!

I haven't gone up here yet...

Wow!

Hello!

You have found the Heavenly Observatory!
Make yerself comfy!

Don't mind if I do.
Plomp!

Lie back and relax.
Ahh... Such a nice view!

Check it out! We are one with the universe!
I do feel pretty special here.

Big E would really dig it! He would call this place magical.

And Tony... he'd like how dark and secret this place is.
He'd also dig all the pillows!

I wish they were here. It's no fun without them.

Oh? But it looks to me like you've been having lots of fun.

Gee, I guess I have!

Things are all right, Full Moon Night.
indeed!

LTK!! Is that YOU?
WAH!

TONY!
I've been looking all over for you!
Didja miss me?

Well, yeah! Who else would I show all these cool prizes to?

Look! I got a star wand, and a rubber duckie...
Me, too!
Ha-ha! Copy cat!

Too bad Big E couldn't come aboard. He'd have won lots of prizes, too.
Except for the trampoline prize.
Imagine Big E on that teeny weeny thing!
HA HA HA HA HA HA!
bye-bye happy cats

Your attention, please! The magic show is just about to begin!
This way, please

I wish Big E could be here.
I do, too.
have a seat

Big E's nuts for magic!
You lookin' fer yer friend?
eep!
Hi!
Hi!
Hi!

Aw, are you shy around dogs? I don't bite!
Kitty 'fraid!

Please welcome MR. MAGICUS!
clap clap clap!
clap clap clap!

OBSERVE!

shuuup!
I SHALL PLACE MY **HAT** DOWN HERE!

And Huzzah! MAKE THIS **RABBIT** APPEAR!
clap! clap! clap!

GO NOW, RABBIT! INTO THE **BOX**!
AND BE **CLASPED** IN TIGHT BY **TWELVE SOLID LOCKS**!
click!
click!
clack!
gasp!
ooh!

LET'S GO FOR A **SPIN**!
SO WE CAN SEE **ALL** THE SIDES!
woooooooo!

And VOILA! NOW THERE ARE...
A **DOZEN SMALL FRIES**!
clap clap clap!
clap clap clap!

This guy is AMAZING!
How does he do it?
clap! clap!
clap!
clap! clap!

FOR MY NEXT TRRRICK I WILL NEED TWO VOLUNTEERS!

Ooh, me! ME!
Pick ME!

Ooh! Pick us both--!
woof!
Ka-POOF

WE HAVE ONE DARING AND ONE BRAVE NOW BEFORE YOU ON STAGE!
clap clap clap clap clap
clap clap
clap!

TAKE A BOW, M'BOYS!
clap clap clap clap

DID YOU LIKE THAT **TRICK**? I HAVE ONE **MORE**!
Mrow!

IT'S **BIGGER** AND **GRANDER** THAN THE ONES BEFORE!
(Get ready!)

CAN YOU **KITTIES** PLEASE HELP ME...
yes Sir!
You bet!

WITH MY **HAT**
you betcha!

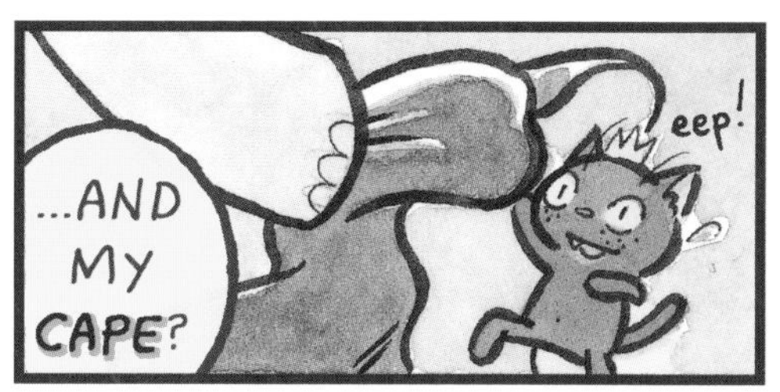
...AND MY **CAPE**?
eep!

AND NOW FOR THE MAGIC WORDS... **PACHYDERMUS MAXIMUS!**
flip!
HONK!
squish!

NO MORE MR. MAGICUS! AN **ELEPHANT** NOW STANDS BEFORE US!
oh!
ha!
clap!
clap!
clap!!

Wow, he really got an elephant up on stage!
clap!
clap!
clap!

Oh no! That means there's an elephant on the Roboboat!

You've been a **TERRIFIC** audience! Thank you and **GOOD NIGHT**!
Quick! Get him!
KA-POOF!

BIG E!
BIG E!
BIG E!
ha!
Dagnabbit! He's escaped onto the deck!

You did it, Big E! You made it aboard!

Hurry! He's getting away!
Go, Mr. Magicus!

Come back here!
I mean, DON'T come back here!!!
BIGE! BIGE! BIGE!
ha! ha! ha!

Your magic show was the best!
And we thought you were going to miss it!

Miss my own show? Never!
nuh-uh!
I had to show off my tricks!

Paws down, tonight's best prize was your surprise!

My favorite kind!

HOW BIG E SNUCK ONTO THE ROBOBOAT

no elephants!
Robobarker bars the entrance,
splish
splish
so Big E swims to the end of the boat...
...and sneaks on board!
where's the elephant?
what elephant?
He watches for security.
toss a rock!
Pok!
mebbe he's over there.
He creates a diversion!
or mayb
not!
He avoids being seen!
okay, back to work, I guess.
Yessir.
He waits until the coast is clear.
He squeezes through a door...
... that leads to a dressing room.
nope!
He tries on a costume...
nuh-uh!
...and tries on another...
YES!
and then finds the perfect one!

The Birthday Present

LONG TAIL KITTY!
I'm coming!

I'm almost done!
Hurry up!

Ready!
patta
patta
patta
patta
Gee, took you long enough!

P'shaw! You didn't have to wait for me.
Sure I did! You'd be lost getting to the party on your own.

That's not true!
Okay. It's probably true.

So, wanna see my PRESENT? Guess what it is!
boink!
BIG is what it is.

I made it myself!
That's why it took so long!
Uh huh.

Can I see your present?
Nope!

Why not? C'mon, Tony!
Nuh-uh! It's not all fancy like yours.

It's the thought that counts, Tony.
yer just sayin' that
hoo!

I can't wait to give Big E my present.
hi mistah

Speaking of Big E, where is he hiding?
your present is TiNY!

Look out below, animals!

BAH - BAH
BAP - DAH!
WHOOOSH!
Oh, BIG E!

The birthday boy... has ARRIVED!
A PERFECT LANDING!

Happy Birthday, Big E! You can open my present now!

Oh, thanks! But I couldn't open it now. The party has only just begun!
?

Everyone, please gather 'round! I am DELIGHTED you are here!
It's just sitting there.

We'll play GAMES! We'll SING! We'll DANCE and eat lots of CAKE!
What about presents?
ULP!

Without further ado, let us begin! FRANCES will hand out the batons!
I'm Frances!
ZING!
Never mind the batons! Big E didn't open my present, Tony!

He just put it down with all the others! Why, oh why? I want him to open it!
Being shy!
One for you!

What did you say?
Och! You're not even listening to me!
swish!
One for you....
woosh

Hey, pay attention! Get your game faces on, boys! FOCUS!!
Coach of all forest animals

All right!! NOW we're all on the same page!
RRR.
RRR.
RAWR!

Gather 'round!

Ready... SET... GO!

wak!
smack!
wok!

Boink!
This way, Turtle!
whoosh!

SMACK!
Double Punch!

AND ALL AT ONCE...
CRACK!
WHOA! Rainbow Peanuts!!
Oh!
yeep!
Hah!
Woot!

Whoa, LTK! You're making record time!
CATCH! CATCH! CATCH!
fwip!

IMPRESSIVE!
DONE! What's next?
I pumped you up...
...too much.
whoa.
INDEED.

Are presents next?
WAP!
ack!
Let's have presents next!
May I have this one?

Everyone please gather your peanuts..!
Because Chubby Bunny is next!

Presents are NOT next.
Ahem! Are we ready?
flop!
I said, ARE we **READY** for Chubby Bunny???
Huh? Oh! Yes, I am ready!
Where are your peanuts?
Take this and get going!

Gah! You all started without me!
Chubby Bunny! Chubby Bunny!
You must say it three times!
Dems da rules!

Chubby Bunny!
Chubby Bunny!
Chubby Bunny!
23 PEANUTS!
21 PEANUTS!
Whooo will win?

How about me? Am I the winner?
um...
hm...
Only 2 peanuts!
hooo...

It looks like the squirrels are the winners !
ulp!
wow.
50 PEANUTS EACH !
o my cheeks!

HOORAY! We have twin winners! But now it's time for presents.

LTK, you shouted with yer mouth full, and look what happened.
Oops.
Also, it is not time for presents yet.

It is time now for ... SINGING!
Oh, yes. Singinnng.
I like singing.

I like singing, too!
ZING!
Winners lead the song!
have a palette cleanser!

Oh, please hurry and sing the song.
Are you a good singer?
Help!
Me Me Me
Gargle!

Happy Birthday~
Make a wish!
Basso
Soprano

Cut the cake and grab a dish!
Be the first to fill your cup
Give a cheer now bottom's up!

Happy Birthday
Here's your chance!
Take the stage and do a dance!

Stomp your heels!
And tap your toes!

Clap your paws!

Honk someone's nose!
gotchu!
ZING!

Honk Happy Birthday, for Elephant!
We love ya truly
you're excellent!

Thank you!
yay!
Thank you!

Now that we've played games...
yam yam
Sung and eaten cake...
yummy!

I think it's time for presents!
HOORAY!
wow, someone is really excited.

Eenie Meenie
Miney Moe...
In the elephant tradition, I will choose a present.
...please oh please oh please...

... here we go!

Oh! That's my present!

Ohhhhhh... um...
That's my present.
crying ever so softly!

I played the piñata game. I collected peanuts. I played Chubby Bunny. I sang the birthday song. I drank punch and ate cake!
Yer bein' scary, LTK.

Now I must watch Big E open your present.
Oho! Frowning at my party?

Please don't be sad, LTK. I will open your present.
Really?

I will open ALL the presents!
yay!

One per day!
That's crazy!

To take one's time for appreciation is my elephant way.
Another custom of mine is ...
He's driving me crazy.

...giving gifts to friends
yay!
That's more like it!

PRESENTUS
MAGICUS

AMAZING!
whoopee!

A sapling! I love my present, Big E. Thank you!

And I will open your present soon, LTK. I promise!

You are my dear friend.
Happy Birthday, Big E!
I want a hug now
me too!
BEAR HUG!

THE PRESENT THAT LTK GAVE TO BIG E

Big E opens his present.
oh!
It's a TIN CAN PHONE SET!
I'll call LTK!
flap flap flap
A call for you!
Hello? This is LTK!
Hi, LTK! I opened your present!
I love it!

HOORRRAY!!!

<Big E?>
<Big E?>

I hear you loud and clear, little buddy.

A Long Walk Home

That was the BEST party ever!

It was EXCITING! It was DRAMATIC! It was FULL of SURPRISES!

You bet it was! Big E picked my present, and everyone got mad!
Frances wasn't mad.

Really?

She LIKES you!
HO! HO! HO!

How can she like me? We're not even friends yet.
Aw, making friends is easy.

Don't tease, LTK! I'm really bad at making friends.
Oh, Tony. You're being so serious.
flop!

Just because you're good at something doesn't mean I'm good at it, too.
But I'm telling you, it's EASY!

You think everything is easy! How about finding your own way home? Bet that's easy!
MROW!
flop again!

Good Luck!
Tony!
...

Please come back! I'm lost without you!
The trees all look the same!
I'm walking in circles!

Oh, Tony, is that you?
rustle rustle

GOTCHA!
OH?

Oh! You aren't Tony. You are Frances!
And you're.. Long Tail Kitty, yes?
yep.

Are you headed this way?
Um... Sort of?
I have no clue where I'm going!

I was with Tony, but he ran off.
Tony, the cute red kitty?
Did he get spooked?

Maybe these woods are too much for him.
Nah-uh! Tony knows these parts like the back of his paw!
Unlike me! I can get lost in a closet.

He ran off to teach me a lesson, but I'll show him! I'll find my OWN way.
That's the spirit!

CRIIIIICK!
WAUGH!
Oh my goodness!

What is it? What is it?!
I don't know! I can't see!
hop!

Wow, yer a skittish kitty... a Long Tail Skitty!
oh.
ha!
Gimme a hug!

Aw, you got me, Froggie!
How about it, Mr. Frog? Want to show LT Skitty around?

Give me a tour, please!
HOPPITY HOP HOP!
hop

This spot is Fuzzy Top.
The grass looks so nice and soft!

On-ward!

whoa.
zzz...
This here cave is Big Mouth! Sometimes you can hear it talking! (It seems to be asleep right now.)

And this spot is Juuust Right.
Ahh...

It's so different from where I live. But... it's not so bad!
Not scared anymore?

Call me BRITTY! That's short for Brave Kitty!

Oh, wait up!
C'mon, Britty! We're almost there.

Where are we...
Oh!

Ta-dah!

I rent a room on the second floor.

I'll wave to you from my window.
Okay, I'll wave back!

Hmm. I walked with Frances, all the way back to her house.
But I forgot! I have to go home, too!

büp büp
büp

büp
Home sweet home!

Long Tail Kitty, do you know the way back?
Not at all.

I can draw you a map!
I would like that very much, please.

Catch!

I got it!
I got it!
fwip!

WE MET HERE
FUZZY TOP
BIG MOUTH
JUST RIGHT
ME (FRANCES)
Oh, good. I remember all these places.

I just have to find them again.

Hot diggety! I sat here!
Things're going Juuuust Right!

Hmm..
And this is the cave that talks... Big Mouth!

Ahem! The talking credit goes NOT to the cave...

...but to ME! I am... THE VOICE!

the very FRIENDLY VOICE!
Gah! A BAT!
Oh, SKITTY!

huff!
I... made it to...
...Fuzzy Top!
huff! huff!
huff!
huff!
huff!
huff!

aw nuts
SPLUT!!

Fuzzy Top, I'm afraid to say you have quite a squishy, muddy bottom.

Must... get to... dry... land!

Woooo. I made it in one piece.

This must be the spot where I met Frances.

There are no more landmarks on the map.
I'm all on my own again!

I wish I had a map that showed me where Tony is.

Maybe I'll spot him from the top of this hill.

Is that a rock or the back of a cat's head?

It's a cat's head!
It's Tony's head!

Heya, LTK.
Tony, you waited for me!

That I did! Where ya been?
All over! I got lost right away.

Still, you made it back in one piece. Congratulations!
Oh, I had help! LOTS of help.

So... if you're not mad anymore, can you walk me home?
Sure.
I have a favor to ask, too.

Think you can help me with making friends?
Lemme see...

It's a DEAL!

All Together Now

You shoulda seen me! I was really lost!

Well, I'm glad to hear you are home now!

Hold on a sec, LTK. The squirrels are winning...
yes!
a fierce tug-o-war battle!
Hah!

Ha-HAH! Now I'm winning!
ack!
NO!

Ooh, you sound busy. We can talk again later.

Well, Pet Fishie...
clunk.

I'm going outside for some quiet time.

doo
doo
doo

ssshh!

sprinkle
sprinkle

pff~
pff

ah...

mmm.

yawn!

zzz...

Hey!
poke!
huh?

My baby tree is wilted and in dire need of help.
You need to plant it, Tony!

Can I plant it here? I don't have a yard.
'Cos you live in an alley!
I like my alley!

Are you sure they can't be planted closer together?
They'll get closer as they grow bigger.

Kinda like you and me!
Corny cat.
hyuk-hyuk!

Yoohooooo! Long Tail Britty!
HONK!
RRRRTT!
HONK!
HONK!
ZING!

Ready to make friends?
Say yes!
No!
Okay.

Surprise visit, kitties!
Hey-ho! Hullabaloo at LTK's house!
Hello, Britty!

So you've been busy watering the plants?
You bet! They were thirsty!
Oh, we're thirsty, too!
zing

Got anything to drink--
WAH!
eep!
Sure! We've got--
Tony, what?!
We've got water!
mini spritz!
WATER FIGHT!

Whose side are you on, LTK?
I'm on Tony's side!
ah...
uh...
um...

I DUNNOOOOOOO!
LTK took too long to decide!
Innocent bystander down!
HO! HO!
gonna getchu!
HAH!
HA!

Ack! Watch the saplings! And the flowers! And the veggies! And MY PET ROCKS!

Play along, Long Tail Kitty!
Yeah, more running! Less watching!

Ha Ha Ha!
Hurry up and catch each other already!
(my rocks!)
boop!
HO! HO!
mrow!

Can't catch us!
We're fleet on our feet!

OOF!
WUMP!!

WAAAH!
blah.
ow.
oh.

Does this yard have room for one more?

...Big E! You appeared out of the blue!
How did you get here?

with MAGIC of COURSE!
ah!
fwooomp!
magic...
of coooourse

I'm officially soaked!
Me, too.
Me three.
Me spinning.

Here, a gentle breeze!
I'm next!
once again
D R Y
No, me!

Next!
wheee!
You're okay, little trees.

Back in your tower, rocks!

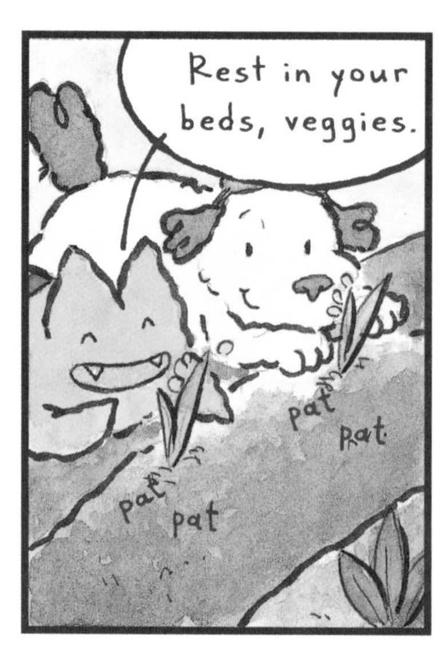
Rest in your beds, veggies.
pat
pat
pat
pat

I wound the water hose back up!
Thank you!

Your friends are crazy, LTK!
My friends are YOUR friends, Frances!
want a flower?
Hey!
sure!

I uh... would like a flower, too.
Oh! I'll get you one.

I think she likes me!
You needed no help!
pluck!
BOP!

whisper
whisper
Hey! We want flowers, too!
Officially Tired!

GAH!! Why are dere f'owers in muh noze??
'Cos we ALL get flowers, ha!!
clap!
clap!
clap!
SNORT!
Smells super nice, right?
yes!
Gotcha!

Oh, it's getting late.
yakity yak!
ha-ha!

It's been a real riot with you kids.
More!
Yeah, more!
There'll be MORE tomorrow!
(There better be!)

Want a ride to your place in the city, Tony?
C'mon, Red! Say yes!
Yes, please!
Atta Boy!

I'll take Frances back home.
Long Tail Kitty knows where I live!
Want to give me directions, LTK?
um...

Good night, my friends!
VROOM!
Whee!
POOF!

I'm back, Fishie!

My alone time turned into EVERYBODY time!
yawn!
Can you believe it?

But now it's just you and me time!

nom nom nom... You look so yummy!

Ha-ha! Don't worry, Pet Fishie. I'd never eat you.

How about a story? I can read to you.

We'll begin with the first chapter.

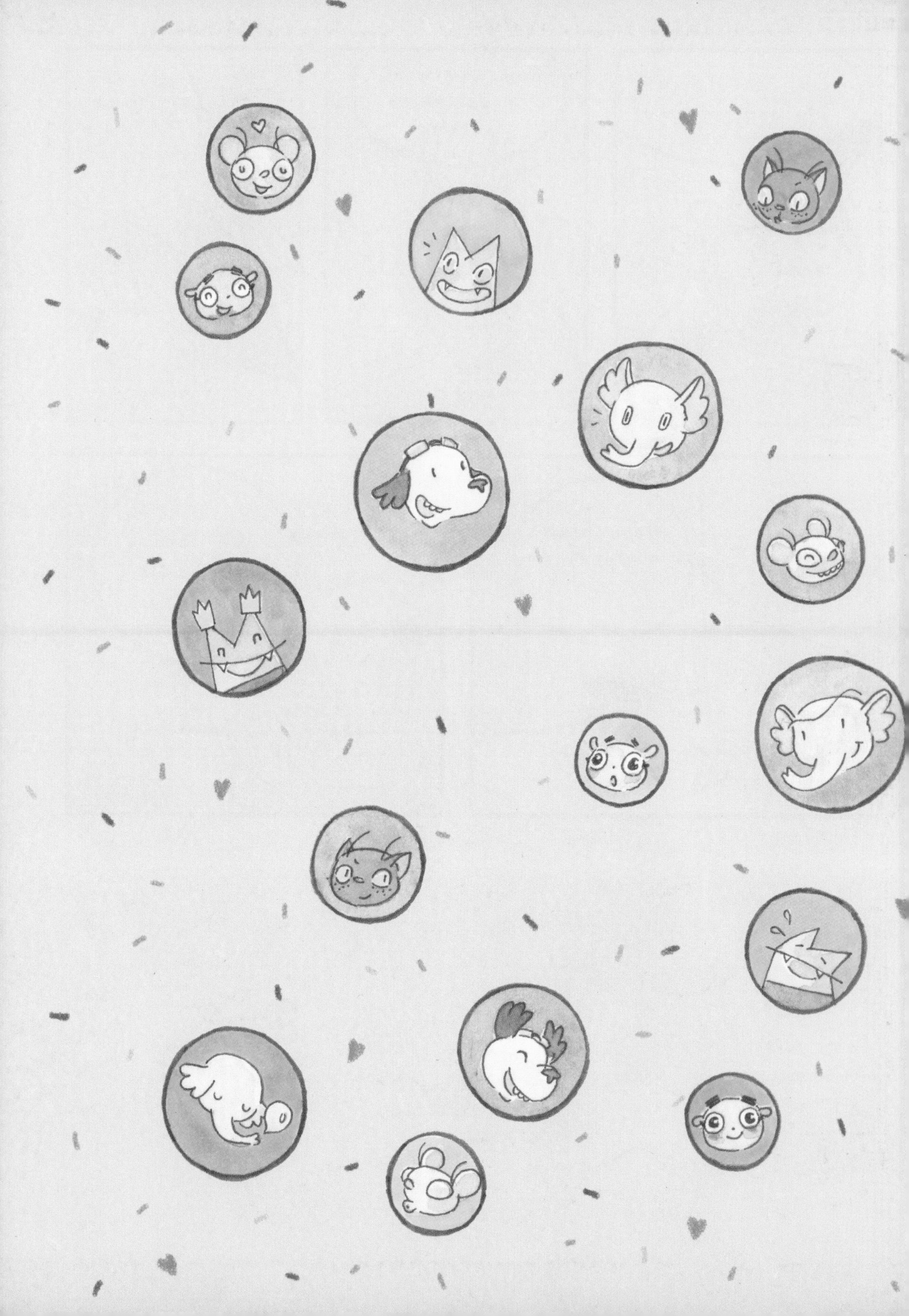